The Inside Of The Cup

Volume 8

Winston Churchill

The Inside Of The Cup, Vol 8.

Winston Churchill

PO Box 2211
Fairfield, IA 52556
www.1stworldlibrary.org
First Edition

LCCN: 2003099820

Softcover ISBN: 1-59540-146-6
Hardcover ISBN: 1-4218-0696-7
eBook ISBN: 1-59540-196-2

The Inside Of The Cup, Vol 8.

contributed by Ed, Tim & Rodney

in support of

1st World Library Literary Society

TABLE OF CONTENTS

Volume 8

CHAPTER XXVII

RETRIBUTION

I

The Bishop's House was a comfortable, double dwelling of a smooth, bright red brick and large, plate-glass windows, situated in a plot at the western end of Waverley Place. It had been bought by the Diocese in the nineties, and was representative of that transitional period in American architecture when the mansard roof had been repudiated, when as yet no definite types had emerged to take its place. The house had pointed gables, and a tiny and utterly useless porch that served only to darken the front door, made of heavy pieces of wood fantastically curved.

It was precisely ten o'clock in the morning when Hodder rang the bell and was shown into the ample study which he had entered on other and less vital occasions. He found difficulty in realizing that this pleasant room, lined with well-worn books and overlooking a back lawn where the clothes of the episcopal family hung in the yellow autumn sun, was to be his judgment seat, whence he might be committed to trial for heresy.

And this was the twentieth century! The full force of the preposterous fact smote him, and a consciousess of the distance he himself had travelled since the comparatively recent days of his own orthodoxy. And suddenly he was full again of a resentful impatience, not only that he should be called away from his labours, his cares, the strangers who were craving his help, to answer charges of such an absurd triviality, but that the performance of the great task to which he had set his hand, with God's help, should depend upon it. Would his enemies be permitted to drive him out thus easily?

The old bishop came in, walking by the aid of a cane. He smiled at Hodder, who greeted him respectfully, and bidding him sit down, took a chair himself behind his writing table, from whence he gazed awhile earnestly and contemplatively at the rugged features and strong shoulders of the rector of St. John's. The effect of the look was that of a visual effort to harmonize the man with the deed he had done, the stir he had created in the city and the diocese; to readjust impressions.

A hint of humour crept into the bishop's blue eyes, which were watery, yet strong, with heavy creases in the corners. He indicated by a little gesture three bundles of envelopes, bound by rubber bands, on the corner of his blotter.

"Hodder," he said, "see what a lot of trouble you have made for me in my old age! All those are about you."

The rector's expression could not have been deemed stern, but it had met the bishop's look unflinchingly. Now it relaxed into a responding smile, which was not without seriousness.

"I am sorry, sir," Hodder answered, "to have caused you any worry - or inconvenience."

"Perhaps," said the bishop, "I have had too much smooth sailing for a servant of Christ. Indeed, I have come to that conclusion."

Hodder did not reply. He was moved, even more by the bishop's manner and voice than his words. And the opening to their conversation was unexpected. The old man put on his spectacles, and drew from the top of one of the bundles a letter.

"This is from one of your vestrymen, Mr. Gordon Atterbury," he said, and proceeded to read it, slowly. When he had finished he laid it down.

"Is that, according to your recollection, Mr. Hodder, a fairly accurate summary of the sermon you gave when you resumed the pulpit at the end of the summer?"

"Yes, sir," answered the rector, "it is surprisingly accurate, with the exception of two or three inferences which I shall explain at the proper moment."

"Mr. Atterbury is to be congratulated on his memory," the bishop observed a little dryly. "And he has saved me the trouble of reading more. Now what are the inferences to which you object?"

Hodder stated them. "The most serious one," he added, "is that which he draws from my attitude on the virgin birth. Mr. Atterbury insists, like others who cling to that dogma, that I have become what he vaguely calls an Unitarian. He seems incapable of grasping my meaning, that the only true God the age knows, the world has ever known, is the

God in Christ, is the Spirit in Christ, and is there not by any material proof, but because we recognize it spiritually. And that doctrine and dogma, ancient speculations as to how, definitely, that spirit came to be in Christ, are fruitless and mischievous to-day. Mr. Atterbury and others seem actually to resent my identification of our Lord's Spirit with the social conscience as well as the individual conscience of our time."

The bishop nodded.

"Hodder," he demanded abruptly, leaning forward over his desk, "how did this thing happen?"

"You mean, sir - "

There was, in the bishop's voice, a note almost pathetic. "Oh, I do not mean to ask you anything you may deem too personal. And God forbid, as I look at you, as I have known you, that I should doubt your sincerity. I am not your inquisitor, but your bishop and your friend, and I am asking for your confidence. Six months ago you were, apparently, one of the most orthodox rectors in the diocese. I recognize that you are not an impulsive, sensational man, and I am all the more anxious to learn from your own lips something of the influences, of the processes which have changed you, which have been strong enough to impel you to risk the position you have achieved."

By this unlooked-for appeal Hodder was not only disarmed, but smitten with self-reproach at the thought of his former misjudgment and under-estimation of the man in whose presence he sat. And it came over him, not only the extent to which, formerly, he had regarded the bishop as too tolerant and easygoing, but the fact that he had arrived here today prepared to find in his superior anything but the attitude he was showing. Considering the bishop's age, Hodder had been ready for a lack of understanding of the step he had taken, even for querulous reproaches and rebuke.

He had, therefore, to pull himself together, to adjust himself to the unexpected greatness of soul with which he was being received before he began to sketch the misgivings he had felt from the early days of his rectorship of St. John's; the help-lessness and failure which by degrees had come over him. He related how it had become apparent to him that by far the greater part of his rich and fashionable congregation were Christians only in name, who kept their religion in a small and impervious compartment where it did not interfere with their lives. He pictured the yearning and perplexity of those who had come to him for help, who could not accept the old explanations, and had gone away empty; and he had not been able to make Christians of the poor who attended the parish house. Finally, trusting in the bishop's discretion, he spoke of the revelations he had unearthed in Dalton Street, and how these had completely destroyed his confidence in the Christianity he had preached, and how he had put his old faith to the test of unprejudiced modern criticism, philosophy, and science. . .

The bishop listened intently, his head bent, his eyes on he rector.

"And you have come out - convinced?" he asked tremulously. "Yes, yes, I see you have. It is enough."

He relapsed into thought, his wrinkled hand lying idly on the table.

"I need not tell you, my friend," he resumed at length, "that a great deal of pressure has been brought to bear upon me in this matter, more than I have ever before experienced. You have mortally offended, among others, the most powerful layman in the diocese, Mr. Parr, who complains that you have presumed to take him to task concerning his private affairs."

"I told him," answered Holder, "that so long as he continued to live the life he leads, I could not accept his contributions to St. John's."

"I am an old man," said the bishop, "and whatever usefulness I have had is almost finished. But if I were young to-day, I should pray God for the courage and insight you have shown, and I am thankful to have lived long enough to have known you. It has, at least, been given one to realize that times have changed, that we are on the verge of a mighty future. I will be frank to say that ten years ago, if this had happened, I should have recommended you for trial. Now I can only wish you God-speed. I, too, can see the light, my friend. I can see, I think, though dimly, the beginnings of a blending of all sects, of all religions in the increasing vision of the truth revealed in Jesus Christ, stripped, as you say, of dogma, of fruitless attempts at rational explanation. In Japan and China, in India and Persia, as well as in Christian countries, it is coming, coming by some working of the Spirit the mystery of which is beyond us. And nations and men who even yet know nothing of the Gospels are showing a willingness to adopt what is Christ's, and the God of Christ."

Holder was silent, from sheer inability to speak.

"If you had needed an advocate with me," the bishop continued, "you could not have had one to whose counsel I would more willingly have listened, than that of Horace Bentley. He wrote asking to come and see me, but I went to him in Dalton Street the day I returned. And it gives me satisfaction, Mr. Holder, to confess to you freely that he has taught me, by his life, more of true Christianity than I have learned in all my experience elsewhere."

"I had thought," exclaimed the rector, wonderingly, "that I owed him more than any other man."

"There are many who think that - hundreds, I should say," the bishop replied . . . . "Eldon Parr ruined him, drove him from the church.... It is strange how, outside of the church, his influence has silently and continuously grown until it has borne fruit in - this. Even now," he added after a pause, "the cautiousness, the dread of change which comes with old age might, I think, lead me to be afraid of it if I - didn't perceive behind it the spirit of Horace Bentley."

It struck Holder, suddenly, what an unconscious

but real source of confidence this thought had likewise been to him. He spoke of it.

"It is not that I wouldn't trust you," the bishop went on. "I have watched you, I have talked to Asa Waring, I have read the newspapers. In spite of it all, you have kept your head, you have not compromised the dignity of the Church. But oh, my friend, I beg you to bear in mind that you are launched upon deep waters, that you have raised up many enemies - enemies of Christ - who seek to destroy you. You are still young. And the uncompromising experiment to which you are pledged, of freeing your church, of placing her in the position of power and influence in the community which is rightfully hers, is as yet untried. And no stone will be left unturned to discourage and overcome you. You have faith, - you have made me feel it as you sat here, - a faith which will save you from bitterness in personal defeat. You may not reap the victory, or even see it in your lifetime. But of this I am sure, that you will be able to say, with Paul, "I have planted, Apollos watered, but God gave the increase." Whatever happens, you may count upon my confidence and support. I can only wish that I were younger, that my arm were stronger, and that I had always perceived the truth as clearly as I see it now."

Holder had risen involuntarily while these words were being spoken. They were indeed a benediction, and the intensity of his feeling warned him of the inadequacy of any reply. They were pronounced in sorrow, yet in hope, and they brought home to him, sharply, the nobility of the bishop's own sacrifice.

"And you, sir?" he asked. "Ah," answered the bishop, "with this I shall have had my life. I am content. . . ."

"You will come to me again, Hodder? some other day," he said, after an interval, "that we may talk over the new problems. They are constructive, creative, and I am anxious to hear how you propose to meet them. For one thing, to find a new basis for the support of such a parish. I understand they have deprived you of your salary."

"I have enough to live on, for a year or so," replied the rector, quickly. "Perhaps more."

"I'm afraid," said the bishop, with a smile in his old eyes, "that you will need it, my friend. But who can say? You have strength, you have confidence, and God is with you."

II

Life, as Hodder now grasped it, was a rapidly whirling wheel which gave him no chance to catch up with the impressions and experiences through which it was dragging him. Here, for instance, were two far-reaching and momentous events, one crowding upon the other, and not an hour for reflection, realization, or adjustment! He had, indeed, after his return from the bishop's, snatched a few minutes to write Alison the unexpected result of that interview. But even as he wrote and rang for a messenger to carry the note to Park Street, he was conscious of an effort to seize upon and hold the fact that the woman he had so intensely desired was now his helpmate; and had, of her own freewill, united herself with him. A strong sense of the dignity of their relationship alone prevented his calling her on the telephone - as it doubtless had prevented her. While she remained in her father's house, he could not. . .

In the little room next to the office several persons were waiting to see him. But as he went downstairs he halted on the, landing, his hand going to his forehead, a reflex movement significant of a final attempt to achieve the hitherto unattainable feat of imagining her as his wife. If he might only speak to her again - now, this morning! And yet he knew that he needed no confirmation. The reality was there, in the background; and though refusing to come forward to be touched, it had already grafted itself as an actual and vital part of his being, never to be eliminated.

Characteristically perfecting his own ideal, she had come to him in the hour when his horizon had been most obscure. And he experienced now an exultation, though solemn and sacred, that her faith had so far been rewarded in the tidings he now confided to the messenger. He was not, as yet, to be driven out from the task, to be deprived of the talent, the opportunity intrusted to him by Lord - the emancipation of the parish of St. John's.

The first to greet him, when he entered his office, was one who, unknown to himself, had been fighting the battle of the God in Christ, and who now, thanks to John Hodder, had identified the Spirit as the transforming force. Bedloe Hubbell had come to offer his services to the Church. The tender was unqualified.

"I should even be willing, Mr. Hodder," he said with a smile, "to venture occasionally into a pulpit. You have not only changed my conception of religion, but you have made it for me something which I can now speak about naturally."

Hodder was struck by the suggestion.

"Ah, we shall need the laymen in the pulpits, Mr. Hubbell," he said quickly. "A great spiritual movement must be primarily a lay movement. And I promise you you shall not lack for opportunity."

III

At nine o'clock that evening, when a reprieve came, Hodder went out. Anxiety on the score of Kate Marcy, as well as a desire to see Mr. Bentley and tell him of the conversation with the bishop, directed his steps toward Dalton Street. And Hodder had, indeed, an intention of confiding to his friend, as one eminently entitled to it, the news of his engagement to Alison Parr.

Nothing, however, had been heard of Kate. She was not in Dalton Street, Mr. Bentley feared. The search of Gratz, the cabinet-maker, had been fruitless. And Sally Grover had even gone to see the woman in the hospital, whom Kate had befriended, in the hope of getting a possible clew. They sat close together before the fire in Mr. Bentley's comfortable library, debating upon the possibility of other methods of procedure, when a carriage was heard rattling over the pitted asphalt without. As it pulled up at the curb, a silence fell between them. The door-bell rang.

Holder found himself sitting erect, rigidly attentive, listening to the muffled sound of a woman's voice in the entry. A few moments later came a knock at the library door, and Sam entered.

The old darky was plainly frightened.

"It's Miss Kate, Marse Ho'ace, who you bin tryin' to fin'," he stammered.

Holder sprang to his feet and made his way rapidly around the table, where he stood confronting the woman in the doorway. There she was, perceptibly swaying, as though the floor under her were rocked by an earthquake. Her handsome face was white as chalk, her pupils widened in terror. It was curious, at such an instant, that he should have taken in her costume, - yet it was part of the mystery. She wore a new, close-fitting, patently expensive suit of dark blue cloth and a small hat, which were literally transforming in their effect, demanding a palpable initial effort of identification.

He seized her by the arm.

"What is it?" he demanded.

"Oh, my God!" she cried. "He - he's out there - in the carriage."

She leaned heavily against the doorpost, shivering . . . . Holder saw Sally Grover coming down the stairs.

"Take her," he said, and went out of the front door, which Sam had left open. Mr. Bentley was behind him.

The driver had descended from the box and was peering into the darkness of the vehicle when he heard them, and turned. At sight of the tall clergyman, an expression of relief came into his face.

"I don't like the looks of this, sir," he said. "I thought he was pretty bad when I went to fetch him - "

Holder pushed past him and looked into the carriage. Leaning back, motionless, in the corner of the seat was the figure of a man. For a terrible moment of premonition, of enlightenment, the rector gazed at it.

"They sent for me from a family hotel in Ayers Street," the driver was explaining. Mr. Bentley's voice interrupted him.

"He must be brought in, at once. Do you know where Dr. Latimer's office is, on Tower Street?" he asked the man. "Go there, and bring this doctor back with you as quickly as possible. If he is not in, get another, physician."

Between them, the driver and Holder got the burden out of the carriage and up the steps. The light from the hallway confirmed the rector's fear.

"It's Preston Parr," he said.

The next moment was too dreadful for surprise, but never had the sense of tragedy so pierced the innermost depths of Holder's being as now, when Horace Bentley's calmness seemed to have forsaken him; and as he gazed down upon the features on the pillow, he wept . . . . Holder turned away. Whatever memories those features evoked, memories of a past that still throbbed with life these were too sacred for intrusion. The years of exile, of uncomplaining service to others in this sordid street and over the wide city had not yet sufficed to allay the pain, to heal the wound of youth. Nay, loyalty had kept it fresh - a loyalty that was the handmaid of faith. . .

The rector softly left the room, only to be confronted with another harrowing scene in the library, where a frantic woman was struggling in Sally Grover's grasp. He went to her assistance. . . Words of comfort, of entreaty were of no avail, - Kate Marcy did not seem to hear them. Hers, in contrast to that other, was the unmeaning grief, the overwhelming sense of injustice of the child; and with her regained physical strength the two had all they could do to restrain her.

"I will go to him," she sobbed, between her paroxysms, "you've got no right to keep me - he's mine . . . he came back to me - he's all I ever had. . . ."

So intent were they that they did not notice Mr. Bentley standing beside them until they heard his voice.

"What she says is true," he told them. "Her place is in there. Let her go."

Kate Marcy raised her head at the words, and looked at him a strange, half-comprehending, half-credulous gaze. They released her, helped her towards the bedroom, and closed the door gently behind her. . . The three sat in silence until the carriage was heard returning, and the doctor entered.

The examination was brief, and two words, laconically spoken, sufficed for an explanation - apoplexy, alcohol. The prostrate, quivering woman was left where they had found her.

Dr. Latimer was a friend of Mr. Bentley's, and

betrayed no surprise at a situation which otherwise might have astonished him. It was only when he learned the dead man's name, and his parentage, that he looked up quickly from his note book.

"The matter can be arranged without a scandal," he said, after an instant. "Can you tell me something of the circumstances?"

It was Hodder who answered.

"Preston Parr had been in love with this woman, and separated from her. She was under Mr. Bentley's care when he found her again, I infer, by accident. From what the driver says, they were together in a hotel in Ayers Street, and he died after he had been put in a carriage. In her terror, she was bringing him to Mr. Bentley."

The doctor nodded.

"Poor woman!" he said unexpectedly. "Will you be good enough to let Mr: Parr know that I will see him at his house, to-night?" he added, as he took his departure.

IV

Sally Grower went out with the physician, and it was Mr. Bentley who answered the question in the rector's mind, which he hesitated to ask.

"Mr. Parr must come here," he said.

As the rector turned, mechanically, to pick up his hat, Mr. Bentley added

"You will come back, Hodder?"

"Since you wish it, sir," the rector said.

Once in the street, he faced a predicament, but swiftly decided that the telephone was impossible under the circumstances, that there could be no decent procedure without going himself to Park Street. It was only a little after ten. The electric car which he caught seemed to lag, the stops were interminable. His thoughts flew hither and thither. Should he try first to see Alison? He was nearest to her now of all the world, and he could not suffer the thought of her having the news otherwise. Yes, he must tell her, since she knew nothing of the existence of Kate Marcy.

Having settled that, - though the thought of the blow she was to receive lay like a weight on his heart, - Mr. Bentley's reason for summoning Eldon Parr to Dalton Street came to him. That the feelings of Mr. Bentley towards the financier were those of Christian forgiveness was not for a moment to be doubted: but a meeting, particularly under such circumstances, could not but be painful indeed. It must be, it was, Hodder saw, for Kate Marcy's sake; yes, and for Eldon Parr's as well, that he be given this opportunity to deal with the woman whom he had driven away from his son, and ruined.

The moon, which had shed splendours over the world the night before, was obscured by a low-drifting mist as Hodder turned in between the ornamental lamps that marked the gateway of the Park Street mansion, and by some undiscerned thought - suggestion he pictured the heart-broken woman he had left beside the body of one who had been heir to all this magnificence. Useless now, stone and iron and glass, pictures and statuary. All the labour, all the care and cunning, all the stealthy planning to get ahead of others had been in vain! What indeed were left to Eldon Parr! It was he who needed pity, - not the woman who had sinned and had been absolved because of her great love; not the wayward, vice-driven boy who lay dead.

The very horror of what Eldon Parr was now to suffer turned Hodder cold as he rang the bell and listened for the soft tread of the servant who would answer his summons.

The man who flung open the door knew him, and did not conceal his astonishment.

"Will you take my card to Miss Parr," the rector said, "if she has not retired, and tell her I have a message?"

"Miss Parr is still in the library, sir."

"Alone?"

"Yes, sir." The man preceded him, but before his name had been announced Alison was standing, her book in her hand, gazing at him with startled eyes, his name rising, a low cry, to her lips.

"John!"

He took the book from her, gently, and held her hands.

"Something has happened!" she said. "Tell me - I can bear it."

He saw instantly that her dread was for him, and it made his task the harder.

It's your brother, Alison."

"Preston! What is it? He's done something - "

Hodder shook his head.

"He died - to-night. He is at Mr. Bentley's."

It was like her that she did not cry out, or even speak, but stood still, her hands tightening on his, her breast heaving. She was not, he knew, a woman who wept easily, and her eyes were dry. And he had it to be thankful for that it was given him to be with her, in this sacred relationship, at such a moment. But even now, such was the mystery that ever veiled her soul, he could not read her feelings, nor know what these might be towards the brother whose death he announced.

"I want to tell you, first, Alison, to prepare you," he said.

Her silence was eloquent. She looked up at him bravely, trustfully, in a way that made him wince. Whatever the exact nature of her suffering, it was too deep for speech. And yet she helped him, made it easier for him by reason of her very trust, once given not to be withdrawn. It gave him a paradoxical understanding of her which was beyond definition.

"You must know - you would have sometime to know that there was a woman he loved, whom he intended to marry - but she was separated from him. She was not what is called a bad woman, she was a working girl. I found her, this summer, and she told me the story, and she has been under the care of Mr. Bentley. She disappeared two or three days ago. Your brother met her again, and he was stricken with apoplexy while with her this evening. She brought him to Mr. Bentley's house."

"My father - bought her and sent her away."

"You knew?"

"I heard a little about it at the time, by accident. I have always remembered it . . . . I have always felt that something like this would happen."

Her sense of fatality, another impression she gave of living in the deeper, instinctive currents of life, had never been stronger upon him than now. . . . She released his hands.

"How strange," she said, "that the end should have come at Mr. Bentley's! He loved my mother - she was the only woman he ever loved."

It came to Hodder as the completing touch of the revelation he had half glimpsed by the bedside.

"Ah," he could not help exclaiming, "that explains much."

She had looked at him again, through sudden tears, as though divining his reference to Mr. Bentley's grief, when a step make them turn. Eldon Parr had entered the room. Never, not even in that last interview, had his hardness seemed so concretely apparent as now. Again, pity seemed never more out of place, yet pity was Hodder's dominant feeling as he met the coldness, the relentlessness of the glance. The thing that struck him, that momentarily kept closed his lips, was the awful, unconscious timeliness of the man's entrance, and his unpreparedness to meet the blow that was to crush him.

"May I ask, Mr. Hodder," he said, in an unemotional voice, "what you are doing in this house?"

Still Hodder hesitated, an unwilling executioner.

"Father," said Alison, "Mr. Hodder has come with a message."

Never, perhaps, had Eldon Parr given such complete proof of his lack of spiritual intuition. The atmosphere, charged with presage for him, gave him nothing.

"Mr. Hodder takes a strange way of delivering it," was his comment.

Mercy took precedence over her natural directness. She laid her hand gently on his arm. And she had, at that instant, no thought of the long years he had neglected her for her brother.

"It's about - Preston," she said.

"Preston!" The name came sharply from Eldon Parr's lips. "What about him? Speak, can't you?"

"He died this evening," said Alison, simply.

Hodder plainly heard the ticking of the clock on the mantel . . . .And the drama that occurred was the more horrible because it was hidden; played, as it were, behind closed doors. For the spectators, there was only the black wall, and the silence. Eldon Parr literally did nothing,- made no gesture, uttered no cry. The death, they knew, was taking place in his soul, yet the man stood before them, naturally, for what seemed an interminable time . .

"Where is he?" he asked.

"At Mr. Bentley's, in Dalton Street." It was Alison who replied again.

Even then he gave no sign that he read retribution in the coincidence, betrayed no agitation at the mention of a name which, in such a connection, might well have struck the terror of judgment into his heart. They watched him while, with a firm step, he crossed the room and pressed a button in the wall, and waited.

"I want the closed automobile, at once," he said, when the servant came.

"I beg pardon; sir, but I think Gratton has gone to bed. He had no orders."

"Then wake him," said Eldon Parr, "instantly. And send for my secretary."

With a glance which he perceived Alison comprehended, Hodder made his way out of the room. He had from Eldon Parr, as he passed him, neither question, acknowledgment, nor recognition. Whatever the banker might have felt, or whether his body had now become a mere machine mechanically carrying on a life-long habit of action, the impression was one of the tremendousness of the man's consistency. A great effort was demanded to summon up the now almost unimaginable experience of his confidence; of the evening when, almost on that very spot, he had revealed to Hodder the one weakness of his life. And yet the effort was not to be, presently, without startling results. In the darkness of the street the picture suddenly grew distinct on the screen of the rector's mind, the face of the banker subtly drawn with pain as he had looked down on it in compassion; the voice with its undercurrent of agony:

"He never knew how much I cared - that what I was doing was all for him, building for him, that he might carry on my work."

V

So swift was the trolley that ten minutes had elapsed, after Hodder's arrival, before the purr of an engine and the shriek of a brake broke the stillness of upper Dalton Street and announced the stopping of a heavy motor before the door. The rector had found Mr. Bentley in the library, alone, seated with bent head in front of the fire, and had simply announced the intention of Eldon Parr to come. From the chair Hodder had unobtrusively chosen, near the window, his eyes rested on the noble profile of his friend. What his thoughts were, Hodder could not surmise; for he seemed again, marvellously, to have regained the outward peace which was the symbol of banishment from the inner man of all thought of self.

"I have prepared her for Mr. Parr's coming," he said to Hodder at length.

And yet he had left her there! Hodder recalled the words Mr. Bentley had spoken, "It is her place." Her place, the fallen woman's, the place she had earned by a great love and a great renunciation, of which no earthly power might henceforth deprive her . . . .

Then came the motor, the ring at the door, the entrance of Eldon Parr into the library. He paused, a perceptible moment, on the threshold as his look fell upon the man whom he had deprived of home and fortune, - yes and of the one woman in the world for them both. Mr. Bentley had risen, and stood facing him. That shining, compassionate gaze should have been indeed a difficult one to meet. Vengeance was the Lord's, in truth! What ordeal that Horace Bentley in anger and retribution might have devised could have equalled this!

And yet Eldon Parr did meet it - with an effort. Hodder, from his corner, detected the effort, though it were barely discernible, and would have passed a scrutiny less rigid, - the first outward and visible sign of the lesion within. For a brief instant the banker's eyes encountered Mr. Bentley's look with a flash of the old defiance, and fell, and then swept the room.

"Will you come this way, Mr. Parr?" Mr. Bentley said, indicating the door of the bedroom.

Alison followed. Her eyes, wet with unheeded tears, had never left Mr. Bentley's face. She put out her hand to him . . . .

Eldon Parr had halted abruptly. He knew from

Alison the circumstances in which his son had died, and how he had been brought hither to this house, but the sight of the woman beside the bed fanned into flame his fury against a world which had cheated him, by such ignominious means, of his dearest wish. He grew white with sudden passion.

"What is she doing here?" he demanded.

Kate Marcy, who had not seemed to hear his entrance, raised up to him a face from which all fear had fled, a face which, by its suggestive power, compelled him to realize the absolute despair clutching now at his own soul, and against which he was fighting wildly, hopelessly. It was lying in wait for him, With hideous patience, in the coming watches of the night. Perhaps he read in the face of this woman whom he had condemned to suffer all degradation, and over whom he was now powerless, something which would ultimately save her from the hell now yawning for him; a redeeming element in her grief of which she herself were not as yet conscious, a light shining in the darkness of her soul which in eternity would become luminous. And he saw no light for him - He thrashed in darkness. He had nothing, now, to give, no power longer to deprive. She had given all she possessed, the memorial of her kind which would outlast monuments.

It was Alison who crossed the room swiftly. She laid her hand protectingly on Kate Marcy's shoulder, and stooped, and kissed her. She turned to her father.

"It is her right," she said. "He belonged to her, not to us. And we must take her home with us.

"No," answered Kate Marcy' "I don't want to go. I wouldn't live," she added with unexpected intensity, "with him."

"You would live with me," said Alison.

"I don't want to live!" Kate Marcy got up from the chair with an energy they had not thought her to possess, a revival of the spirit which had upheld her when she had contended, singly, with a remorseless world. She addressed herself to Eldon Parr. "You took him from me, and I was a fool to let you. He might have saved me and saved himself. I listened to you when you told me lies as to how it would ruin him . . . . Well, - I had him you never did."

The sudden, intolerable sense of wrong done to her love, the swift anger which followed it, the justness of her claim of him who now lay in the dignity of death clothed her - who in life had been crushed and blotted out - with a dignity not to be gainsaid. In this moment of final self-assertion she became the dominating person in the room, knew for once the birthright of human worth. They watched her in silence as she turned and gave one last, lingering look at the features of the dead; stretched out her hand towards them, but did not touch them . . . and then went slowly towards the door. Beside Alison she stopped.

"You are his sister?" she said.

"Yes."

She searched Alison's face, wistfully.

"I could have loved you."

"And can you not - still?"

Kate Mercy did not answer the question.

"It is because you understand," she said. "You're like those I've come to know - here. And you're like him. . . . I don't mean in looks. He, too, was good - and square." She spoke the words a little defiantly, as though challenging the verdict of the world. "And he wouldn't have been wild if he could have got going straight."

"I know," said Alison, in a low voice.

"Yes," said Kate Mercy, "you look as if you did. He thought a lot of you, he said he was only beginning to find out what you was. I'd like you to think as well of me as you can."

"I could not think better," Alison replied.

Kate Mercy shook her head.

"I got about as low as any woman ever got," she said

"Mr. Hodder will tell you. I want you to know that I wouldn't marry - your brother," she hesitated over the name. "He wanted me to - he was mad with me to night, because I wouldn't - when this happened."

She snatched her hand free from Alison's, and fled out of the room, into the hallway.

Eldon Parr had moved towards the bed, seemingly unaware of the words they had spoken. Perhaps, as he gazed upon the face, he remembered in his agony the sunny, smiling child who need to come hurrying down the steps in Ransome Street to meet him.

In the library Mr. Bentley and John Hodder, knowing nothing of her flight, heard the front door close on Kate Marcy forever . . . .

CHAPTER XXVIII

LIGHT

I

Two days after the funeral, which had taken place from Calvary, and not from St. John's, Hodder was no little astonished to receive a note from Eldon Parr's secretary requesting the rector to call in Park Street. In the same mail was a letter from Alison. "I have had," she wrote, "a talk with my father. The initiative was his. I should not have thought of speaking to him of my affairs so soon after Preston's death. It seems that he strongly suspected our engagement, which of course I at once acknowledged, telling him that it was your intention, at the proper time, to speak to him yourself.

"I was surprised when he said he would ask you to call. I confess that I have not an idea of what he intends to say to you, John, but I trust you absolutely, as always. You will find him, already, terribly changed. I cannot describe it - you will see for yourself. And it has all seemed to happen so suddenly. As I wrote you, he sat up both nights, with Preston - he could not be induced to leave the room. And after the first night he was different. He has hardly spoken a word, except when he sent for me this evening, and he eats nothing . . . . And yet, somehow, I do not think that this will be the end. I feel that he will go on living. . . . .

"I did not realize how much he still hoped about Preston. And on Monday, when Preston so unexpectedly came home, he was happier than I have known him for years. It was strange and sad that he could not see, as I saw, that whatever will power my brother had had was gone. He could not read it in the face of his own son, who was so quick to detect it in all others! And then came the tragedy. Oh, John, do you think we shall ever find that girl again? - I know you are trying but we mustn't rest until we do. Do you think we ever shall? I shall never forgive myself for not following her out of the door, but, I thought she had gone to you and Mr. Bentley."

Hodder laid the letter down, and took it up again. He knew that Alison felt, as he felt, that they never would find Kate Marcy . . . . He read on.

"My father wished to speak to me about the money. He has plans for much of it, it appears, even now. Oh. John, he will never understand. I want so much to see you, to talk to you - there are times when I am actually afraid to be alone, and without you. If it be weakness to confess that I need your reassurance, your strength and comfort constantly, then I am weak. I once thought I could stand alone, that I had solved all problems for myself, but I know now how foolish I was. I have been face to face with such dreadful, unimagined things, and in my ignorance I did not conceive that life held such terrors. And when I look at my father, the thought of immortality turns me faint. After you have come here this afternoon there can be no longer any reason why we should not meet, and all the world know it. I will go with you to Mr. Bentley's.

"Of course I need not tell you that I refused to inherit anything. But I believe I should have consented if I possibly could have done so. It seemed so cruel - I can think of no other word - to have, to refuse at such a moment. Perhaps I have been cruel to him all my life - I don't know. As I look back upon everything, all our relations, I cannot see how I could have been different. He wouldn't let me. I still believe to have stayed with him would have been a foolish and useless sacrifice . . .

But he looked at me so queerly, as though he, too, had had a glimmering of what we might have been to each other after my mother died. Why is life so hard? And why are we always getting glimpses of things when it is too late? It is only honest to say that if I had it to do all over again, I should have left him as I did.

"It is hard to write you this, but he actually made the condition of my acceptance of the inheritance that I should not marry you. I really do not believe I convinced him that you wouldn't have me take the money under any circumstances. And the dreadful side of it all was that I had to make it plain to him - after what has happened that my desire to marry you wasn't the main reason of my refusal. I had to tell him that even though you had not been in question, I couldn't have taken what he wished to give me, since it had not been honestly made. He asked me why I went on eating the food bought with such money, living under his roof? But I cannot, I will not leave him just yet . . . It is two o'clock. I cannot write any more to-night."

II

The appointed time was at the November dusk, hurried forward nearly an hour by the falling panoply of smoke driven westward over the Park by the wet east wind. And the rector was conducted, with due ceremony, to the office upstairs which he had never again expected to enter, where that other memorable interview had taken place. The curtains were drawn. And if the green-shaded lamp - the only light in the room - had been arranged by a master of dramatic effect, it could not have better served the setting.

In spite of Alison's letter, Holder was unprepared for the ravages a few days had made in the face of Eldon Parr. Not that he appeared older: the impression was less natural, more sinister. The skin had drawn sharply over the cheek-bones, and strangely the eyes both contradicted and harmonized with the transformation of the features. These, too, had changed. They were not dead and lustreless, but gleamed out of the shadowy caverns into which they had sunk, unyielding, indomitable in torment, - eyes of a spirit rebellious in the fumes

This spirit somehow produced the sensation of its being separated from the body, for the movement of the hand, inviting Holder to seat himself, seemed almost automatic.

"I understand," said Eldon Parr, "that you wish to marry my daughter."

"It is true that I am to marry Alison," Holder answered, "and that I intended, later on, to come to inform yon of the fact."

He did not mention the death of Preston. Condolences, under the circumstances, were utterly out of the question.

"How do you propose to support her?" the banker demanded.

"She is of age, and independent of you. You will pardon me if I reply that this is a matter between ourselves," Holder said.

"I had made up my mind that the day she married you I would not only disinherit her, but refuse absolutely, to have anything to do with her."

"If you cannot perceive what she perceives, that you have already by your own life cut her off from you absolutely and that seeing her will not mend matters while you remain relentless, nothing I can say will convince you." Holder did not speak rebukingly. The utter uselessness of it was never more apparent. The man was condemned beyond all present reprieve, at least.

"She left me," exclaimed Eldon Parr, bitterly.

"She left you, to save herself."

"We need not discuss that."

"I am far from wishing to discuss it," Holder replied.

"I do not know why you have asked me to come here, Mr. Parr. It is clear that your attitude has not changed since our last conversation. I tried to make it plain to you why the church could not accept your money. Your own daughter, cannot accept it."

"There was a time," retorted the banker, "when you did not refuse to accept it."

"Yes," Holder replied, "that is true." It came to him vividly then that it had been Alison herself who had cast the enlightening gleam which revealed his inconsistency. But he did not defend himself.

"I can see nothing in all this, Mr. Hodder, but a species of insanity," said Eldon Parr, and there crept into his tone both querulousness and intense exasperation. "In the first place, you insist upon marrying my daughter when neither she nor you have any dependable means of support. She never spared her criticisms of me, and you presume to condemn me, a man who, if he has neglected his children, has done so because he has spent too much of his time in serving his community and his country, and who has - if I have to say it myself - built up the prosperity which you and others are doing your best to tear down, and which can only result in the spread of misery. You profess to have a sympathy with the masses, but you do not know them as I do. They cannot control themselves, they require a strong hand. But I am not asking for your sympathy. I have been misunderstood all my life, I have become used to ingratitude, even from my children, and from the rector of the church for which I have done more than any other man."

Hodder stared at him in amazement.

"You really believe that!" he exclaimed.

"Believe it!" Eldon Parr repeated. "I have had my troubles, as heavy bereavements as a man can have. All of them, even this of my son's death, all the ingratitude and lack of sympathy I have experienced - " (he looked deliberately at Hodder) "have not prevented me, do not prevent me to-day from regarding my fortune as a trust. You have deprived St. John's, at least so long as you remain there, of some of its benefits, and the responsibility for that is on your own head. And I am now making arrangements to give to Calvary the settlement house which St. John's should have had."

The words were spoken with such an air of conviction, of unconscious plausibility, as it were, that it was impossible for Hodder to doubt the genuineness of the attitude they expressed. And yet it was more than his mind could grasp . . . . Horace Bentley, Richard Garvin, and the miserable woman of the streets whom he had driven to destroy herself had made absolutely no impression whatever! The gifts, the benefactions of Eldon Parr to his fellow-men would go on as before!

"You ask me why I sent for you," the banker went on. "It was primarily because I hoped to impress upon you the folly of marrying my daughter. And in spite of all the injury and injustice you have done me, I do not forget that you were once in a relationship to me which has been unique in my life. I trusted you, I admired you, for your ability, for your faculty of getting on with men. At that time you were wise enough not to attempt to pass comment upon accidents in business affairs which are, if deplorable, inevitable."

Eldon Parr's voice gave a momentary sign of breaking.

"I will be frank with you. My son's death has led me, perhaps weakly, to make one more appeal. You have ruined your career by these chimerical, socialistic notions you have taken up, and which you mistake for Christianity. As a practical man I can tell you, positively, that St. John's will run downhill until you are bankrupt. The people who come to you now are in search of a new sensation, and when that grows stale they will fall away. Even if a respectable number remain in your congregation, after this excitement and publicity have died down, I have reason to know that it is impossible to support a large city church on contributions. It has been tried again and again, and failed. You have borrowed money for the Church's present needs. When that is gone I predict that you will find it difficult to get more."

This had every indication of being a threat, but Hodder, out of sheer curiosity, did not interrupt. And it was evident that the banker drew a wrong conclusion from his silence, which he may actually have taken for reluctant acquiescence. His tone grew more assertive.

"The Church, Mr. Hodder, cannot do without the substantial business men. I have told the bishop so, but he is failing so rapidly from old age that I might as well not have wasted my breath. He needs an assistant, a suffragan or coadjutor, and I intend to make it my affair to see that he gets one. When I remember him as he was ten years ago, I find it hard to believe that he is touched with these fancies. To be charitable, it is senile decay. He seems to forget what I have done for him, personally, made up his salary, paid his expenses at different times, and no appeal for the diocese to me was ever in vain. But again, I will let that go.

"What I am getting at is this. You have made a mess of the affairs of St. John's, you have made a mess of your life. I am willing to give you the credit for sincerity. Some of my friends might not be. You want to marry my daughter, and she is apparently determined to marry you. If you are sensible and resign from St. John's now I will settle on Alison a sufficient sum to allow you both to live in comfort and decency the rest of your lives. I will not have it said of me that I permitted my daughter to become destitute."

After he had finished, the rector sat for so long a time that the banker nervously shifted in his chair. The clergyman's look had a cumulative quality, an intensity which seemed to increase as the silence continued. There was no anger in it, no fanaticism. On the contrary, the higher sanity of it was disturbing; and its extraordinary implication - gradually borne in upon Eldon Parr - was that he himself were not in his right mind. The words, when they came, were a confirmation of this nference.

"It is what I feared, Mr. Parr," he said. "You are as yet incapable of comprehending."

"What do you mean?" asked the banker, jerking his hand from the table.

The rector shook his head.

"If this great chastisement with which you have been visited has given you no hint of the true meaning of life, nothing I can say will avail. If you will not yet listen to the Spirit which is trying to make you comprehend, how then will you listen to me? How am I to open your eyes to the paradox of truth, that he who would save his life shall lose it, that it is easier for a camel to go through the eye of a needle, than for a rich man to enter into the

Kingdom of God? If you will not believe him who said that, you will not believe me. I can only beg of you, strive to understand, that your heart many be softened, that your suffering soul may be released."

It is to be recorded, strangely, that Eldon Parr did not grow angry in his turn. The burning eyes looked out at Hodder curiously, as at a being upon whom the vials of wrath were somehow wasted, against whom the weapons of power were of no account. The fanatic had become a phenomenon which had momentarily stilled passion to arouse interest. . . "Art thou a master of Israel, and knowest not these things?"

"Do you mean to say" - such was the question that sprang to Eldon Parr's lips - "that you take the Bible literally? What is your point of view? You speak about the salvation of souls, I have heard that kind of talk all my life. And it is easy, I find, for men who have never known the responsibilities of wealth to criticize and advise. I regard indiscriminate giving as nothing less than a crime, and I have always tried to be painstaking and judicious. If I had taken the words you quoted at their face value, I should have no wealth to distribute to-day.

"I, too, Mr. Hodder, odd as it may seem to you,

have had my dreams - ofdoing my share of making this country the best place in the world to live in. It has pleased providence to take away my son. He was not fitted to carry on my work, - that is the way - with dreams. I was to have taught him to build up, and to give, as I have given. You think me embittered, hard, because I seek to do good, to interpret the Gospel in my own way. Before this year is out I shall have retired from all active business.

"I intend to spend the rest of my life in giving away the money I have earned - all of it. I do not intend to spare myself, and giving will be harder than earning. I shall found institutions for research of disease, hospitals, playgrounds, libraries, and schools. And I shall make the university here one of the best in the country. What more, may I ask, would you have me do?"

"Ah," replied the rector, "it is not what I would have you do. It is not, indeed, a question of 'doing,' but of seeing."

"Of seeing?" the banker repeated. "As I say, of using judgment."

"Judgment, yes, but the judgment which has not yet dawned for you, the enlightenment which is the knowledge of God's will. Worldly wisdom is a rule of thumb many men may acquire, the other wisdom, the wisdom of the soul, is personal - the reward of revelation which springs from desire. You ask me what I think you should do. I will tell you - but you will not do it, you will be powerless to do it unless you see it for yourself, unless the time shall come when you are willing to give up everything you have held dear in life, - not your money, but your opinions, the very judgment and wisdom you value, until you have gained the faith which proclaims these worthless, until you are ready to receive the Kingdom of God as a little child. You are not ready, now. Your attitude, your very words, proclaim your blindness to all that has happened you, your determination to carry out, so far as it is left to you, your own will. You may die without seeing."

Crazy as it all sounded, a slight tremor shook Eldon Parr. There was something in the eyes, in the powerful features of the clergyman that kept him still, that made him listen with a fascination which had he taken cognizance of it - was akin to fear. That this man believed it, that he would impress it upon others, nay, had already done so, the banker did not then doubt.

"You speak of giving," Hodder continued, "and

you have nothing to give - nothing. You are poorer to-day than the humblest man who has seen God. But you have much, you have all to restore." Without raising his voice, the rector had contrived to put a mighty emphasis on the word. "You speak of the labour of giving, but if you seek your God and haply find him you will not rest night or day while you live until you have restored every dollar possible of that which you have wrongfully taken from others."

John Hodder rose and raised his arm in effective protest against the interruption Eldon Parr was about to make. He bore him down.

"I know what you are going to say, Mr. Parr, - that it is not practical. That word 'practical' is the barrier between you and your God. I tell you that God can make anything practical. Your conscience, the spirit, tortures you to-day, but you have not had enough torture, you still think to escape easily, to keep the sympathy of a world which despises you. You are afraid to do what God would have you do. You have the opportunity, through grace, by your example to leave the world better than you found it, to do a thing of such magnitude as is given to few men, to confess before all that your life has been blind and wicked. That is what the Spirit is trying to teach you. But you fear the ridicule of the other blind men, you have not the faith to believe that many eyes would be opened by your act. The very shame of such a confession, you think, is not to be borne."

"Suppose I acknowledge, which I do not, your preposterous charge, how would you propose to do this thing?"

"It is very simple," said the rector, "so far as the actual method of procedure goes. You have only to establish a board of men in whom you have confidence, - a court of claims, so to speak, - to pass upon the validity of every application, not from a business standpoint alone, but from one of a broad justice and equity. And not only that. I should have it an important part of the duties of this board to discover for themselves other claimants who may not, for various reasons, come forward. In the case of the Consolidated Tractions, for instances there are doubtless many men like Garvin who invested their savings largely on the strength of your name. You cannot bring him back to life, restore him to his family as he was before you embittered him, but it would be a comparatively easy matter to return to his widow, with compound interest, the sum which he invested."

"For the sake of argument," said Eldon Parr, "what would you do with the innumerable impostors who would overwhelm such a board with claims that they had bought and sold stock at a loss? And that is only one case I could mention."

"Would it be so dreadful a thing," asked Hodder, "To run the risk of making a few mistakes? It would not be business, you say. If you had the desire to do this, you would dismiss such an obsession from your brain, you would prefer to err on the aide of justice and mercy. And no matter how able your board, in making restitution you could at best expect to mend only a fraction of the wrongs you have done."

"I shall waive, for the moment, my contention that the Consolidated Tractions Company, had it succeeded, would greatly have benefited the city. Even if it had been the iniquitous, piratical transaction you suggest, why should I assume the responsibility for all who were concerned in it?"

"If the grace were given you to do this, that question would answer itself," the rector replied. "The awful sense of responsibility, which you now lack, would overwhelm you."

"You have made me out a rascal and a charlatan,"

said Eldon Parr, "and I have listened' patiently in my desire to be fair, to learn from your own lips whether there were anything in the extraordinary philosophy you have taken up, and which you are pleased to call Christianity. If you will permit me to be as frank as you have been, it appears to me as sheer nonsense and folly, and if it were put into practice the world would be reduced at once to chaos and anarchy."

"There is no danger, I am sorry to say, of its being put into practice at once," said Hodder, smiting sadly.

"I hope not," answered the banker, dryly. "Utopia is a dream in which those who do the rough work of the world cannot afford to indulge. And there is one more question. You will, no doubt, deride it as practical, but to my mind it is very much to the point. You condemn the business practices in which I have engaged all my life as utterly unchristian. If you are logical, you will admit that no man or woman who owns stock in a modern corporation is, according to your definition, Christian, and, to use your own phrase, can enter the Kingdom of God. I can tell you, as one who knows, that there is no corporation in this country which, in the struggle to maintain itself, is not forced to adopt the natural law of the survival of the fittest, which you condemn. Your own salary, while you had it, came from men who had made the money in corporations. Business is business, and admits of no sentimental considerations. If you can get around that fact, I will gladly bow to your genius. Should you succeed in reestablishing St. John's on what you call a free basis - and in my opinion you will not - even then the money, you would live on, and which supported the church, would be directly or indirectly derived from corporations."

"I do not propose to enter into an economics argument with you, Mr. Parr, but if you tell me that the flagrant practices indulged in by those who organized the Consolidated Tractions Company can be excused under any code of morals, any conception of Christianity, I tell you they cannot. What do we see today in your business world? Boards of directors, trusted by stockholders, betraying their trust, withholding information in order to profit thereby, buying and selling stock secretly; stock watering, selling to the public diluted values, - all kinds of iniquity and abuse of power which I need not go into. Do you mean to tell me, on the plea that business is business and hence a department by itself, that deception, cheating, and stealing are justified and necessary? The awakened conscience of the public is condemning you.

"The time is at hand, though neither you nor I may live to see it, when the public conscience itself is beginning to perceive thin higher justice hidden from you. And you are attempting to mislead when you do not distinguish between the men who, for their own gain and power, mismanage such corporations as are mismanaged, and those who own stock and are misled.

"The public conscience of which I speak is the leaven of Christianity at work. And we must be content to work with it, to await its fulfilment, to realize that no one of us can change the world, but can only do his part in making it better. The least we can do is to refuse to indulge in practices which jeopardize our own souls, to remain poor if we cannot make wealth honestly. Say what you will, the Christian government we are approaching will not recognize property, because it is gradually becoming clear that the holding of property delays the Kingdom at which you scoff, giving the man who owns it a power over the body of the man who does not. Property produces slavery, since it compels those who have none to work for those who have.

"The possession of property, or of sufficient

property to give one individual an advantage over his fellows is inconsistent with Christianity. Hence it will be done away with, but only when enough have been emancipated to carry this into effect. Hence the saying of our Lord about the needle's eye - the danger to the soul of him who owns much property."

"And how about your Christian view of the world as a vale of tears?" Eldon Parr inquired.

"So long as humanity exists, there will always be tears," admitted the rector. "But it is a false Christianity which does not bid us work for our fellow-men, to relieve their suffering and make the world brighter. It is becoming clear that the way to do this effectively is through communities, cooperation, through nations, and not individuals. And this, if you like, is practical, - so practical that the men like you, who have gained unexampled privilege, fear it more and more. The old Christian misconception, that the world is essentially a bad place, and which has served the ends of your privilege, is going by forever. And the motto of the citizens of the future will be the Christian motto, "I am my brother's keeper." The world is a good place because the Spirit is continually working in it, to make it better. And life is good, if only we take the right view of it, - the revealed view."

"What you say is all very fine," said Eldon Parr. "And I have heard it before, from the discontented, the socialists. But it does not take into account the one essential element, human nature."

"On the other hand, your scheme of life fails to reckon with the greater factor, divine nature," Hodder replied.

"When you have lived as long as I have, perhaps you will think differently, Mr. Hodder." Eldon Parr's voice had abruptly grown metallic, as though the full realization had come over him of the severity of the clergyman's arraignment; the audacity of the man who had ventured to oppose him and momentarily defeated him, who had won the allegiance of his own daughter, who had dared condemn him as an evil-doer and give advice as to his future course. He, Eldon Parr, who had been used to settle the destinies of men! His anger was suddenly at white heat; and his voice, which he strove to control, betrayed it.

"Since you have rejected my offer, which was made in kindness, since you are bent on ruining my daughter's life as well as your own, and she has disregarded my wishes, I refuse to see either of you, no matter to what straits you may come, as long as I live. That is understood. And she leaves this house to-day, never to enter it again. It is useless to prolong this conversation, I think."

"Quite useless, as I feared, Mr. Parr. Do you know why Alison is willing to marry me? It is because the strength has been given me to oppose you in the name of humanity, and this in spite of the fact that her love for you to-day is greater than it has ever been before. It is a part of the heavy punishment you have inflicted on yourself that you cannot believe in her purity. You insist on thinking that the time will come when she will return to you for help. In senseless anger and pride you are driving her away from you whom you will some day need. And in that day, should God grant you a relenting heart to make the sign, she will come to you, - but to give comfort, not to receive it. And even as you have threatened me, I will warn you, yet not in anger. Except a man be born again, he cannot see the Kingdom of God, nor understand the motives of those who would enter into it. Seek and pray for repentance."

Infuriated though he was, before the commanding yet compassionate bearing of the rector he remained speechless. And after a moment's pause, Hodder turned and left the room . . . .

III

When Hodder had reached the foot of the stairs, Alison came out to him. The mourning she wore made her seem even taller. In the face upturned to his, framed in the black veil and paler than he had known it, were traces of tears; in the eyes a sad, yet questioning and trustful smile. They gazed at each other an instant, before speaking, in the luminous ecstasy of perfect communion which shone for them, undimmed, in the surrounding gloom of tragedy. And thus, they felt, it would always shine. Of that tragedy of the world's sin and sorrow they would ever be conscious. Without darkness there could be no light.

"I knew," she said, reading his tidings, "it would be of no use. Tell me the worst."

"If you marry me, Alison, your father refuses to see you again. He insists that you leave the house."

"Then why did he wish to see you?"

"It was to make an appeal. He thinks, of course, that I have made a failure of life, and that if I marry you I shall drag you down to poverty and disgrace."

She raised her head, proudly.

"But he knows that it is I who insist upon marrying you! I explained it all to him - how I had asked you. Of course he did not understand. He thinks, I suppose, that it is simply an infatuation."

In spite of the solemnity of the moment, Hodder smiled down at her, touched by the confession.

"That, my dear, doesn't relieve me of responsibility. I am just as responsible as though I had spoken first, instead of you."

"But, John, you didn't -?" A sudden fear made her silent.

He took her hand and pressed it reassuringly.

"Give you up? No, Alison," he answered simply. "When you came to me, God put you in my keeping."

She clung to him suddenly, in a passion of relief.

"Oh, I never could give you up, I never would unless you yourself told me to. Then I would do it, - for you. But you won't ask me, now?"

He put his arm around her shoulders, and the strength of it seemed to calm her.

"No, dear. I would make the sacrifice, ask you to make it, if it would be of any good. As you say, he does not understand. And you couldn't go on living with him and loving me. That solution is impossible. We can only hope that the time will come when he will realize his need of you, and send for you."

"And did he not ask you anything more?"

Hodder hesitated. He had intended to spare her that . . . Her divination startled him.

"I know, I know without your telling me. He offered you money, he consented to our - marriage if you would give up St. John's. Oh, how could her, she cried. "How could he so misjudge and insult you!"

"It is not me he misjudges, Alison, it is mankind, it is God. That is his terrible misfortune." Hodder released her tenderly. "You must see him - you must tell him that when he needs you, you will come."

"I will see him now, she said. You will wait

for, me?"

"Now?" he repeated, taken aback by her resolution, though it was characteristic.

"Yes, I will go as I am. I can send for my things. My father has given me no choice, no reprieve, - not that I ask one. I have you, dear. I will stay with Mr. Bentley to-night, and leave for New York to-morrow, to do what I have to do - and then you will he ready for me."

"Yes," he said, "I shall be ready."

He lingered in the well-remembered hall . . . . And when at last she came down again her eyes shone bravely through her tears, her look answered the question of his own. There was no need for speech. With not so much as a look behind she left, with him, her father's house.

Outside, the mist had become a drizzle, and as they went down the walk together beside the driveway she slipped her arm into his, pressing close to his side. Her intuition was perfect, the courage of her love sublime.

"I have you, dear," she whispered, "never in my life before have I been rich."

"Alison!"

It was all he could say, but the intensity of his mingled feeling went into the syllables of her name. An impulse made them pause and turn, and they stood looking back together at the great house which loomed the greater in the thickening darkness, its windows edged with glow. Never, as in this moment when the cold rain wet their faces, had the thought of its comfort and warmth and luxury struck him so vividly; yes, and of its terror and loneliness now, of the tortured spirit in it that found no rest.

"Oh, John," she cried, "if we only could!"

He understood her. Such was the perfect quality of their sympathy that she had voiced his thought. What were rain and cold, the inclemency of the elements to them? What the beauty and the warmth of those great, empty rooms to Eldon Parr? Out of the heaven of their happiness they looked down, helpless, into the horrors of the luxury of hell.

"It must be," he answered her, "in God's good time."

"Life is terrible!" she said. "Think of what he must

have done to suffer so, to be condemned to this! And when I went to him, just now, he wouldn't even kiss me good-by. Oh, my dear, if I hadn't had you to take me, what should I have done? . . . It never was a home to me - to any of us. And as I look back now, all the troubles began when we moved into it. I can only think of it as a huge prison, all the more sinister for its costliness."

A prison! It had once been his own conceit. He drew her gently away, and they walked together along Park Street towards the distant arc-light at the corner which flung a gleaming band along the wet pavement.

"Perhaps it was because I was too young to know what trouble was when we lived in Ransome Street," she continued. "But I can remember now how sad my mother was at times - it almost seemed as though she had a premonition." Alison's voice caught . . . .

The car which came roaring through the darkness, and which stopped protestingly at their corner, was ablaze with electricity, almost filled with passengers. A young man with a bundle changed his place in order that they might sit together in one of the little benches bordering the aisle; opposite them was a laughing, clay-soiled group of labourers going home from work; in front, a young couple with a chubby child. He stood between his parents, facing about, gazing in unembarrassed wonder at the dark lady with the veil. Alison's smile seemed only to increase the solemnity of his adoration, and presently he attempted to climb over the barrier between them. Hodder caught him, and the mother turned in alarm, recapturing him.

"You mustn't bother the lady, Jimmy," she said, when she had thanked the rector. She had dimpled cheeks and sparkling blue eyes, but their expression changed as they fell on Alison's face, expressing something of the wonder of the child's.

"Oh, he isn't bothering me," Alison protested. "Do let him stand."

"He don't make up to everybody," explained the mother, and the manner of her speech was such a frank tribute that Alison flushed. There had been, too, in the look the quick sympathy for bereavement of the poor.

"Aren't they nice?" Alison leaned over and whispered to Hodder, when the woman had turned back. "One thing, at least, I shall never regret, - that I shall have to ride the rest of my life in the streetcars. I love them. That is probably my only qualification, dear, for a clergyman's wife."

Hodder laughed. "It strikes me," he said, "as the supreme one."

They came at length to Mr. Bentley's door, flung open in its usual wide hospitality by Sam. Whatever theist fortunes, they would always be welcome here . . . . But it turned out, in answer to their question, that their friend was not at home.

"No, sah," said Sam, bowing and smiling benignantly, "but he done tole me to say, when you and Miss Alison come, hit was to make no diffunce, dat you bofe was to have supper heah. And I'se done cooked it - yassah. Will you kindly step into the liba'y, suh, and Miss Alison? Dar was a lady 'crost de city, Marse Ho'ace said - yassah."

"John," said Alison with a questioning smile, when they were alone before the fire, "I believe he went out on purpose, - don't you? - just that we might be here alone."

"He knew we were coming?"

"I wrote him."

"I think he might be convicted on the evidence,"

Hodder agreed. "But - ?" His question remained unasked.

Alison went up to him. He had watched her, absorbed and fascinated, as with her round arms gracefully lifted in front of the old mirror she had taken off her hat and veil; smoothing, by a few deft touches, the dark crown of her hair. The unwonted intimacy of the moment, invoking as it did an endless reflection of other similar moments in their future life together, was in its effect overwhelming, bringing with it at last a conviction not to be denied. Her colour rose as she faced him, her lashes fell.

"Did you seriously think, dear, that we could have deceived Mr. Bentley? Then you are not as clever as I thought you. As soon as it happened I sent him a note? that very night. For I felt that he ought to be told first of all."

"And as usual," Hodder answered, "you were right."

Supper was but a continuation of that delicious sense of intimacy. And Sam, beaming in his starched shirt and swallow-tail, had an air of presiding over a banquet of state. And for that matter, none had ever gone away hungry from this table, either for meat or love. It was, indeed, a consecrated meal, - consecrated for being just there. Such was the tact which the old darky had acquired from his master that he left the dishes on the shining mahogany board, and bowed himself out.

"When you wants me, Miss Alison, des ring de bell."

She was seated upright yet charmingly graceful, behind the old English coffee service which had been Mr. Bentley's mother's. And it was she who, by her wonderful self-possession, by the reassuring smile she gave him as she handed him his cup, endowed it all with reality.

"It's strange," she said, "but it seems as though I had been doing it all my life, instead of just beginning."

"And you do it as though you had," he declared.

"Which is a proof," she replied, "of the superior adaptability of women."

He did not deny it. He would not then, in truth, have disputed her wildest statement. . . But presently, after they had gone back into the library and were seated side by side before the coals, they spoke again of serious things, marvelling once more at a happiness which could be tinged and yet unmarred by vicarious sorrow. Theirs was the soberer, profounder happiness of gratitude and wonder, too wise to exult, but which of itself is exalted; the happiness which praises, and passes understanding.

"There are many things I want to say to you, John," she told him, once, "and they trouble me a little. It is only because I am so utterly devoted to you that I wish you to know me as I am. I have always had queer views, and although much has happened to change me since I have known and loved you, I am not quite sure how much those views have changed. "Love," she added, "plays such havoc with one's opinions.

She returned his smile, but with knitted brows.

"It's really serious - you needn't laugh. And it's only fair to you to let you know the kind of a wife you are getting, before it is too late. For instance, I believe in divorce, although I can't imagine it for us. One never can, I suppose, in this condition - that's the trouble. I have seen so many immoral marriages that I can't think God intends people to live degraded. And I'm sick and tired of the argument that an indissoluble marriage under all conditions is good for society. That a man or woman, the units of society, should violate the divine in themselves for the sake of society is absurd. They are merely setting an example to their children to do the same thing, which means that society in that respect will never get any better. In this love that has come to us we have achieved an ideal which I have never thought to reach. Oh, John, I'm sure you won't misunderstand me when I say that I would rather die than have to lower it."

"No," he answered, "I shall not misunderstand you."

"Even though it is so difficult to put into words what I mean. I don't feel that we really need the marriage service, since God has already joined us together. And it is not through our own wills, somehow, but through his. Divorce would not only be a crime against the spirit, it would be an impossibility while we feel as we do. But if love should cease, then God himself would have divorced us, punished us by taking away a priceless gift of which we were not worthy. He would have shut the gates of Eden in our faces because we had sinned against the Spirit. It would be quite as true to say 'whom God has put asunder no man may join together.' Am I hurting you?"

Her hand was on the arm of his chair, and the act of laying his own on it was an assurance stronger than words. Alison sighed.

"Yes, I believed you would understand, even though I expressed myself badly, - that you would help me, that you have found a solution. I used to regard the marriage service as a compromise, as a lowering of the ideal, as something mechanical and rational put in the place of the spiritual; that it was making the Church, and therefore God, conform to the human notion of what the welfare of society ought to be. And it is absurd to promise to love. We have no control over our affections. They are in God's hands, to grant or withdraw.

"And yet I am sure - this is new since I have known you - that if such a great love as ours be withdrawn it would be an unpardonable wrong for either of us to marry again. That is what puzzles me - confounds the wisdom I used to have, and which in my littleness and pride I thought so sufficient. I didn't believe in God, but now I feel him, through you, though I cannot define him. And one of many reasons why I could not believe in Christ was because I took it for granted that he taught, among other things, a continuation of the marriage relation after love had ceased to justify it."

Hodder did not immediately reply. Nor did Alison interrupt his silence, but sat with the stillness which at times so marked her personality, her eyes trustfully fixed on him. The current pulsing between them was unbroken. Hodder's own look, as he gazed into the grate, was that of a seer.

"Yes," he said at length, "it is by the spirit and not the letter of our Lord's teaching that we are guided. The Spirit which we draw from the Gospels. And everything written down there that does not harmonize with it is the mistaken interpretation of men. Once the Spirit possesses us truly, we are no longer troubled and confused by texts.

"The alpha and omega of Christ's message is rebirth into the knowledge of that Spirit, and hence submission to its guidance. And that is what Paul meant when he said that it freed us from the law. You are right, Alison, when you declare it to be a violation of the Spirit for a man and woman to live together when love does not exist. Christ shows us that laws were made for those who are not reborn. Laws are the rules of society, to be followed by those who have not found the inner guidance, who live and die in the flesh. But the path which those who live under the control of the Spirit are to take is opened up to them as they journey. If all men and women were reborn we should have the paradox, which only the reborn can understand, of what is best for the individual being best for society, because under the will of the Spirit none can transgress upon the rights and happiness of others. The Spirit would make the laws and rules superfluous.

"And the great crime of the Church, for which she is paying so heavy an expiation, is that her faith wavered, and she forsook the Spirit and resumed the law her Master had condemned. She no longer insisted on that which Christ proclaimed as imperative, rebirth. She became, as you say, a mechanical organization, substituting, as the Jews had done, hard and fast rules for inspiration. She abandoned the Communion of Saints, sold her birthright for a mess of pottage, for worldly, temporal power when she declared that inspiration had ceased with the Apostles, when she failed to see that inspiration is personal, and comes through rebirth. For the sake of increasing her membership, of dominating the affairs of men, she has permitted millions who lived in the law and the flesh, who persisted in forcing men to live by the conventions and customs Christ repudiated, and so stultify themselves, to act in Christ's name. The unpardonable sin against the Spirit is to doubt its workings, to maintain that society will be ruined if it be substituted for the rules and regulations supposed to make for the material comforts of the nations, but which in reality suppress and enslave the weak.

"Nevertheless in spite of the Church, marvellously through the Church the germ of our Lord's message has come down to us, and the age in which we live is beginning to realize its purport, to condemn the Church for her subservient rationalism.

"Let us apply the rule of the Spirit to marriage. If we examine the ideal we shall see clearly that the marriage-service is but a symbol. Like baptism, it is a worthless and meaningless rite unless the man and the woman have been born again into the Spirit, released from the law. If they are still, as St. Paul would say, in the flesh, let them have, if they wish, a civil permit to live together, for the Spirit can have nothing to do with such an union. True to herself, the Church symbolizes the union of her members, the reborn. She has nothing to do with laws and conventions which are supposedly for the good of society, nor is any union accomplished if those whom she supposedly joins are not reborn. If they are, the Church can neither make it or dissolve it, but merely confirm and acknowledge the work of the Spirit. And every work of the Spirit is a sacrament. Not baptism and communion and marriage only, but every act of life.

"Oh, John," she exclaimed, her eyes lighting, "I can believe that! How beautiful a thought! I see now what is meant when it is said that man shall not live by bread alone, but by every word that proceedeth out of the mouth of God. That is the hourly guidance which is independent of the law. And how terrible to think that all the spiritual beauty of such a religion should have been hardened into chapter and verse and regulation. You have put into language what I think of Mr. Bentley, - that has acts are sacraments . . . . It is so simple when you explain it this way. And yet I can see why it was said, too, that we must become as children to understand it."

"The difficult thing," replied Holder, gravely, "is to retain it, to hold it after we have understood it - even after we have experienced it. To continue to live in the Spirit demands all our effort, all our courage and patience and faith. We cannot, as you say, promise to love for life. But the marriage service, interpreted, means that we will use all our human endeavour, with the help of the Spirit, to remain in what may be called the reborn state, since it is by the Spirit alone that true marriage is sanctified. When the Spirit is withdrawn, man and woman are indeed divorced.

"The words 'a sense of duty' belong to moral philosophy and not to religion. Love annuls them. I do not mean to decry them, but the reborn are lifted far above them by the subversion of the will by which our will is submitted to God's. It is so we develop, and become, as it were, God. And hence those who are not married in the Spirit are not spiritually man and wife. No consecration has taken place, Church or no Church. If rebirth occurs later, to either or both, the individual conscience - which is the Spirit, must decide whether, as regards each other, they are bound or free, and we must stand or fall by that. Men object that this is opening the door to individualism. What they fail to see is that the door is open, wide, to-day and can never again be closed: that the law of the naturally born is losing its power, that the worn-out authority of the Church is being set at naught because that authority was devised by man to keep in check those who were not reborn. The only check to material individualism is spiritual individualism, and the reborn man or woman cannot act to the detriment of his fellow-creatures."

In her turn she was silent, still gazing at him, her breath coming deeply, for she was greatly moved.

"Yes," she said simply, "I can see now why divorce between us would be a sacrilege. I felt it, John, but I couldn't reason it out. It is the consecration of the Spirit that justifies the union of the flesh. For the Spirit, in that sense, does not deny the flesh."

"That would be to deny life," Hodder replied.

"I see. Why was it all so hidden!" The exclamation was not addressed to him - she was staring pensively into the fire. But presently, with a swift movement, she turned to him.

"You will preach this, John, - all of it!"

It was not a question, but the cry of a new and wider vision of his task. Her face was transfigured. And her voice, low and vibrating, expressed no doubts. "Oh, I am proud of you! And if they put you out and persecute you I shall always be proud, I shall never know why it was given me to have this, and to live. Do you remember saying to me once that faith comes to us in some human form we love? You are my faith. And faith in you is my faith in humanity, and faith in God."

Ere he could speak of his own faith in her, in mankind, by grace of which he had been lifted from the abyss, there came a knock at the door. And even as they answered it a deeper knowledge filtered into their hearts.

Horace Bentley stood before them. And the light from his face, that shone down upon them, was their benediction.

AFTERWORD

Although these pages have been published serially, it is with a feeling of reluctance that I send them out into the world, for better or worse, between the covers of a book. They have been written with reverence, and the reading of the proofs has brought back to me vividly the long winters in which I pondered over the matter they contain, and wrote and rewrote the chapters.

I had not thought to add anything to them by way of an afterword. Nothing could be farther from my mind than to pose as a theologian; and, were it not for one or two of the letters I have received, I should have supposed that no reader could have thought of making the accusation that I presumed to speak for any one except myself. In a book of this kind, the setting forth of a personal view of religion is not only unavoidable, but necessary; since, if I wrote sincerely, Mr. Hodder's solution must coincide with my own - so far as I have been able to work one out. Such as it is, it represents many years of experience and reflection. And I can only crave the leniency of any trained theologian who may happen to peruse it.

No one realizes, perhaps, the incompleteness of the religious interpretations here presented more keenly than I. More significant, more vital elements of the truth are the rewards of a mind which searches and craves, especially in these days when the fruit of so many able minds lies on the shelves of library and bookshop. Since the last chapter was written, many suggestions have come to me which I should like to have the time to develop for this volume. But the nature of these elements is positive, - I can think of nothing I should care to subtract.

Here, then, so far as what may be called religious doctrine is concerned, is merely a personal solution. We are in an age when the truth is being worked out through many minds, a process which seems to me both Christian and Democratic. Yet a gentleman has so far misunderstood this that he has already accused me, in a newspaper, of committing all the heresies condemned by the Council of Chalcedon, - and more!

I have no doubt that he is right. My consolation

must be that I have as company - in some of my heresies, at least - a goodly array of gentlemen who wear the cloth of the orthodox churches whose doctrines he accuses me of denying. The published writings of these clergymen are accessible to all. The same critic declares that my interpretations are without "authority." This depends, of course; on one's view of "authority." But his accusation is true equally against many men who - if my observation be correct - are doing an incalculable service for religion by giving to the world their own personal solutions, interpreting Christianity in terms of modern thought. No doubt these, too, are offending the champions of the Council of Chalcedon.

And does the gentleman, may I ask, ever read the pages of the Hibbert Journal?

Finally, I have to meet a more serious charge, that Mr. Hodder remains in the Church because of "the dread of parting with the old, strong anchorage, the fear of anathema and criticism, the thought of sorrowing and disapproving friends." Or perhaps he infers that it is I who keep Mr. Hodder in the Church for these personal reasons. Alas, the concern of society is now for those upon whom the Church has lost her hold, who are seeking for a solution they can accept. And the danger to-day is not from the side of heresy. The rector of St. John's, as a result of his struggle, gained what I believe to be a higher and surer faith than that which he formerly held, and in addition to this the realization of the presence of a condition which was paralyzing the Church's influence.

One thing I had hoped to make clear, that if Mr. Hodder had left the Church under these circumstances he would have made the Great Refusal. The situation which he faced demanded something of the sublime courage of his Master.

Lastly, may I be permitted to add that it is far from my intention to reflect upon any particular denomination. The instance which I have taken is perhaps a pronounced rather than a particular case of the problem to which I have referred, and which is causing the gravest concern to thoughtful clergymen and laymen of all denominations.

WINSTON CHURCHILL

SANTA BARBARA, CALIFORNIA
March 31,1913.

Notes

Notes

Notes

Notes

Notes

Notes

Notes

Notes

Notes

Notes

Notes

Notes

Notes

H. Irving Hancock
H. Rider Haggard
H. W. C. Davis
Hamilton Wright Mabie
Hans Christian Andersen
Harold Avery
Harold McGrath
Harriet Beecher Stowe
Harry Houidini
Helent Hunt Jackson
Helen Nicolay
Hendrik Conscience
Hendy David Thoreau
Henri Barbusse
Henrik Ibsen
Henry Adams
Henry Ford
Henry Frost
Henry James
Henry Jones Ford
Henry Seton Merriman
Henry W Longfellow
Herbert A. Giles
Herbert N. Casson
Herman Hesse
Homer
Honore De Balzac
Horace Walpole
Horatio Alger Jr.
Howard Pyle
Howard R. Garis
Hugh Lofting
Hugh Walpole
Humphry Ward
Ian Maclaren
Inez Haynes Gillmore
Irving Bacheller
Israel Abrahams
Ivan Turgenev
J.G.Austin
J. Henri Fabre
J. M. Barrie
J. Macdonald Oxley
J. S. Fletcher
J. S. Knowles
J. Storer Clouston
Jack London
Jacob Abbott
James Allen
James Andrews
James Baldwin
James DeMille
James Joyce
James Lane Allen
James Lane Allen
James Oliver Curwood
James Oppenheim
James Otis
James R. Driscoll
Jane Austen
Jens Peter Jacobsen
Jerome K. Jerome
John Burroughs
John Cournos
John F. Kennedy
John Gay
John Glasworthy
John Habberton
John Joy Bell
John Kendrick Bangs
John Milton
John Philip Sousa
Jonas Lauritz Idemil Lie
Jonathan Swift
Joseph A. Altsheler
Joseph Carey
Joseph Conrad
Joseph E. Badger Jr
Joseph Hergesheimer
Joseph Jacobs
Julian Hawthrone
Julies Vernes
Justin Huntly McCarthy
Kakuzo Okakura
Kenneth Grahame
Kenneth McGaffey
Kate Langley Bosher
Kate Langley Bosher
Katherine Cecil Thurston
Katherine Stokes
L. A. Abbot
L. T. Meade
L. Frank Baum
Latta Griswold
Laura Lee Hope
Laurence Housman
Leo Tolstoy
Leonid Andreyev
Lewis Carroll
Lilian Bell
Lloyd Osbourne
Louis Tracy
Louisa May Alcott
Lucy Fitch Perkins
Lucy Maud Montgomery
Lydia Miller Middleton
Lyndon Orr
M. Corvus
M. H. Adams
Margaret E. Sangster
Margaret Vandercook
Margret Penrose
Maria Edgeworth
Maria Thompson Daviess
Mariano Azuela
Marion Polk Angellotti
Mark Overton
Mark Twain
Mary Austin
Mary Catherine Crowley
Mary Cole
Mary Hastings Bradley
Mary Roberts Rinehart
Mary Rowlandson
M. Wollstonecraft Shelley
Maud Lindsay
Max Beerbohm
Myra Kelly
Nathaniel Hawthrone
Nicolo Machiavelli
O. F. Walton
Oscar Wilde
Owen Johnson
P.G. Wodehouse
Paul and Mabel Thorne
Paul G. Tomlinson
Paul Severing
Percy Brebner
Peter B. Kyne
Plato
R. Derby Holmes
R. L. Stevenson
R. S. Ball
Rabindranath Tagore
Rahul Alvares
Ralph Henry Barbour
Ralph Waldo Emmerson
Rene Descartes
Rex Beach
Rex E. Beach
Richard Harding Davis
Richard Jefferies
Richard Le Gallienne

Robert Barr
Robert Frost
Robert Gordon Anderson
Robert L. Drake
Robert Lansing
Robert Lynd
Robert Michael Ballantyne
Robert W. Chambers
Rosa Nouchette Carey
Rudyard Kipling
Samuel B. Allison
Samuel Hopkins Adams
Sarah Bernhardt
Selma Lagerlof
Sherwood Anderson
Sigmund Freud
Standish O'Grady
Stanley Weyman
Stella Benson
Stephen Crane
Stewart Edward White
Stijn Streuvels
Swami Abhedananda
Swami Parmananda
T. S. Ackland
T. S. Arthur
The Princess Der Ling
Thomas A. Janvier
Thomas A Kempis
Thomas Anderton
Thomas Bailey Aldrich
Thomas Bulfinch
Thomas De Quincey
Thomas H. Huxley
Thomas Hardy
Thomas More
Thornton W. Burgess
U. S. Grant
Valentine Williams
Various Authors
Victor Appleton
Virginia Woolf
Walter Camp
Walter Scott
Washington Irving
Wilbur Lawton
Wilkie Collins
Willa Cather
Willard F. Baker
William Dean Howells
William le Queux
W. Makepeace Thackeray
William W. Walter
Winston Churchill
Yei Theodora Ozaki
Yogi Ramacharaka
Young E. Allison
Zane Grey

www.ingramcontent.com/pod-product-compliance
Lightning Source LLC
Chambersburg PA
CBHW020547310726
48979CB00008B/1121/J

* 9 7 8 1 4 2 1 8 0 6 9 6 9 *